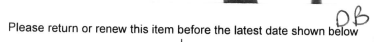

For Arabella, Yasmeen

For my beautiful friend, Ola.
All my love, Lou xx

First published 2019 by Nosy Crow Ltd,
The Crow's Nest, 14 Baden Place, Crosby Row, London SE1 1YW
www.nosycrow.com

ISBN 978 1 78800 402 2 (HB)
ISBN 978 1 78800 401 5 (PB)

Nosy Crow and associated logos are trademarks and/or
registered trademarks of Nosy Crow Ltd.

Text © Lou Peacock 2019
Illustrations © Yasmeen Ismail 2019

The right of Lou Peacock to be identified as the author and of
Yasmeen Ismail to be identified as the illustrator of this work has been asserted.
All rights reserved.

A CIP catalogue record for this book is available from the British Library.

Printed in China
Papers used by Nosy Crow are made from wood grown in sustainable forests.

1 3 5 7 9 8 6 4 2 (HB)
1 3 5 7 9 8 6 4 2 (PB)

Nuts!

Lou Peacock & Yasmeen Ismail

nosy crow

Nuts!
My nuts.

Nuts!
My nuts.

Your
nuts?

My
nuts.

My nuts!

Whose nuts?

His nuts!

Her nuts!

Your nuts . . .

and your nuts.

Our
nuts?

Our
nuts!

Their
nuts!

Apples!

Apples?